OWEN FOOTE, FRONTIERSMAN

OWEN FOOTE, FRONTIERSMAN

by Stephanie Greene

Illustrated by Martha Weston

Clarion Books • New York

Clarion Books
a Houghton Mifflin Company imprint
215 Park Avenue South, New York, NY 10003
Text copyright © 1999 by Stephanie Greene
Illustrations copyright © 1999 by Martha Weston
Cover illustration copyright © 2002 by John Ward

The illustrations were executed in pencil.

Original poem, "Bulb," by Oliver G. Radwan.

www.houghtonmifflinbooks.com

Printed in the USA.

Library of Congress Cataloging-in-Publication Data

Greene, Stephanie.
Owen Foote, frontiersman / by Stephanie Greene ; illustrated by
Martha Weston.
p.   cm.
Summary: Second grader Owen Foote is looking forward to spending
time with his friend Joseph in their tree fort, until some bullies visiting
his neighbor, Mrs. Gold, threaten to wreck the fort.
ISBN 0-395-61578-X   PA ISBN 0-618-24620-7
[1. Tree houses—Fiction. 2. Bullies—Fiction. 3. Mothers and sons—
Fiction. 4. Outdoor life—Fiction.] I. Weston, Martha, ill. II. Title.
PZ7.G8343Ou   1999
[Fic]—dc21
98-44843
CIP   AC

MV 10 9 8 7 6 5 4

Contents

1
This Is My Kingdom!

"Compass?"

"Check."

"Canteen?"

"Check."

"Swiss Army knife?"

"My mother won't let me bring it," Joseph said. "She said I can only use it when my dad's there."

Owen looked at his own Swiss Army knife on the table. "Did you tell her we'll be careful?"

"Yeah. She said it still makes her nervous."

"It's a good thing Daniel Boone didn't have a mother like yours. Hold on a minute."

Owen put down the phone and picked up his hat. He ran his hand over the raccoon tail.

He picked up the phone again. "Hat?"

"You're not going to like this, Owen."

"What happened?"

"Kitty got it. I think she thought it was real. She chewed the tail off."

"Great," Owen said. "Really great."

"My mom said she can sew it back on," Joseph said quickly. "It'll just be a little shorter. Kitty swallowed part of it."

Owen scowled. He and Joseph were supposed to wear their Daniel Boone hats whenever they went into the woods. It was their secret pact.

Owen's mom had given a coonskin cap to every boy who came to Owen's last birthday party. They had all loved them. The fur on the hat part was fake, but the tail was real raccoon.

Owen felt like a pioneer when he wore his.

"Then she threw up on my parents' bed," Joseph said, "so my mom's mad at me."

"Why is she mad at *you*?" said Owen. "You didn't throw up."

"Yeah, but Kitty's my cat and she ate my hat."

"And you're a poet but you don't know it," Owen was tempted to say. But he could tell from Joseph's voice that Joseph didn't feel like joking. Joseph was worried Owen would be mad at him about the hat.

If his mom was already mad at him, he couldn't take much more, Owen knew.

"It's okay," Owen said. "When are you coming over?"

"After I clean my room and practice the violin," said Joseph.

"That'll take forever," said Owen. "I'm going to the fort right now." He looked at his watch. "I'll meet you back here at eleven o'clock, okay?"

"Okay."

"Over and out."

"Over and out," Joseph said. "Bye."

Owen hung up. No matter how many times Owen had told him, Joseph always said "bye" after "over and out."

"Over and out *means* good-bye," Owen said. "It's like you're saying good-bye, good-bye."

But Joseph kept doing it. He told Owen he thought plain "over and out" sounded rude.

Owen and Joseph were best friends. They had known each other since kindergarten. But sometimes Joseph still did the weirdest things. No matter how hard Owen tried to change him.

Owen picked up his backpack and put it over one shoulder. He went to the bottom of the stairs. "I'm going to my fort," he called.

"Okay," his mom called back.

Owen took his animal tracks book from the table and put it in his pack. Most of the pictures showed animal tracks in mud or snow. Today there wasn't any mud or snow outside.

But Owen liked to be prepared. If there were any mountain lions or bears near his fort, he wanted to be ready.

He climbed up onto the kitchen counter and opened the spice cabinet. He took out the jar of red pepper flakes and put it in his pack.

Maybe he couldn't outrun a mountain lion or a bear, but he could at least make it sneeze. Then he'd get away, fast.

He walked across the yard toward the woods. They belonged to an old lady named Mrs. Gold. Her house was way on the other side. She had told Owen he could play in the woods anytime he wanted.

Owen had never told her about his fort. But he didn't think she'd mind. She said her own children had played in the woods all the time. They were grown up now and lived far away. She had told Owen she was glad someone was enjoying the woods as much as her children had.

Owen didn't say it, but he didn't think they could have loved the woods as much as he did. He didn't think anybody could.

Except maybe Daniel Boone.

Owen had read lots of books about Daniel Boone. About how he hunted with a real gun when he was nine. How he could track animals for miles. How he learned to lie so still, deer walked right past him and didn't even know he was there.

In one book Daniel told his mother, "When the forest calls, I have to go."

Owen knew how he felt. When the forest called Owen, he had to go too.

Like now.

He could hear the tops of the pine trees brushing together. And twigs snapping under his feet. As he walked down the path to his fort, he looked around for animal tracks or scat.

Scat was what his track book called animal poop.

It said that between an animal's tracks and its scat, you could read a whole story. About where the animal was going. Whether it was walking or running. What time it had eaten.

Even whether it was sick or healthy.

Owen had studied that book all winter. He had learned how to recognize lots of different tracks. Deer tracks that looked like upside-down hearts. Raccoon tracks that looked like a baby's hand.

Just the way his book said.

At first the only story he could read was that a deer or raccoon had been there. The End.

Then one day he saw a trail of mouse tracks. They made a tiny pattern in the snow like a necklace. He could see where the mouse's tail had dragged. Somehow, Owen could tell that the mouse had been happy.

He had followed the tracks under bushes and across the frozen stream. Then the tracks stopped.

Owen saw a small hole in the snow. There were different, bigger tracks all around it.

Owen saw a tiny splotch of red.

It looked like a drop of bright red paint. But Owen knew it wasn't paint. It was blood.

Mouse blood.

Looking at that bright red spot, Owen could suddenly read the whole story.

A cute little mouse had been skipping along. It was having a wonderful time. It was going home for dinner.

Suddenly there was a low, menacing snarl.

The mouse froze.

A huge, mean animal lunged out of the bushes and landed right in front of the terrified mouse. It bared its sharp teeth.

The little mouse squeaked. Then it started running.

Running for its life.

Its warm, safe house was straight ahead. The little mouse could see the front door.

But it was too late.

The snarling animal pounced. In one bite the happy little mouse was dead.

Only two inches from safety.

It had taught Owen how tracks could tell a story, all right. And that sometimes the story had a bad ending.

Every time Owen thought about that blood, he thought about something else Daniel Boone had said: that the forest was his teacher.

The forest was Owen's teacher too. And even if the lesson wasn't always a happy one, learning it made Owen feel wise.

Today it was sunny and dry. He didn't see a single track. When he got to his fort, he scrambled up the ladder like a monkey. The ladder went straight up, so it was kind of hard for some kids to climb. Especially heavy kids like Joseph.

Joseph was always huffing and puffing so hard by the time he got to the top, Owen wanted to joke and call him "the big bad wolf." But he knew it hurt Joseph's feelings to be kidded about his size.

Owen reached the top and hurled his backpack inside the fort. Then he pulled himself onto the small ledge that ran along the front.

He called it the front porch.

"I don't think it's wide enough to be called a porch," Joseph had said. "There isn't even room for a rocking chair."

But Owen called it that anyway. He liked to name things. That way, he always knew what everything was.

He leaned back against the fort and swung his feet back and forth. There was a window to his right and the opening for the door to his left. Owen took a deep breath and filled his nose with the familiar smell of pine needles.

That's what the roof was made of. Pine branches Owen had cut and put across the top. It was kind of low, so they had to bend over when they were inside. If Joseph stood up, his head could poke right through the roof.

Even Owen's head brushed against the branches if he stood up straight.

But he loved it. It kept out the rain and gave the fort a cozy, green feeling. Owen felt like an animal, safe and sound in its burrow, when he was inside.

He grabbed his pack and crawled over to the old crate they used as their supply box in the far corner. It was where they kept things like comic books, magazines, a deck of cards, and paper and pencils. He opened the top and took out some masking tape. Then he took a piece of paper out of his pack.

It was a poem Joseph had written in school. Mrs. LeDuc had asked them to write poems about nature. She made Joseph read his in front of the whole class. Owen could tell how proud Joseph was by how red his face got.

"Bulb," Joseph read. "Fighting dirt, worms, rodents, and rocks, to be a flower."

They had all waited for more. But that was it.

It was so short, Owen could remember it by heart. He had gone home and copied it in his best cursive. Then he drew pictures of bulbs and flowers and mice around it with his gold pen.

He hadn't told Joseph. He wanted to put it on the fort's Art Wall as a surprise. All they had there now was their secret code and some mazes. They both loved to draw mazes. They had contests to see who could draw the hardest one.

Owen moved the code and their latest mazes to the sides and taped the poem in the middle. Then he turned to look at the Weapons Wall. It had seven spears lined up in straight rows.

Owen had seen a wall like it in a museum. There were about fifty real African spears lined up. They called it African Art. But Owen knew weapons when he saw them.

And if there was one thing a fort needed, it was weapons.

Owen had found all the sticks in the woods and carved the pointy tips himself. He thought they looked pretty dangerous.

His favorite had a huge burl at one end. Owen grabbed it and crawled back out onto the front porch. He stood up and searched the woods for enemies.

Then he raised his spear above his head and shook the burl in the air.

"This is my kingdom!" he shouted.

And nobody around dared to argue.

2

It's Mine

"The whole night?"

"Sure." Owen pushed his way through the brambles that separated his yard from the woods. "It'll be great."

"But there isn't any electricity," Joseph said.

"We don't need electricity. We'll bring flashlights."

"What about a bathroom?"

"We're boys, aren't we? The whole woods are our bathroom."

Joseph's face turned red. "I don't know. It's kind of far away. . . ."

"What do you mean?" Owen bent down to

pull a briar off his jeans. "You can sort of see the corner of our garage if you hold on to the fort and lean out over the front porch, remember? Anyway, my mom said she'll leave the garage light on."

He stood up and looked at Joseph. "You don't want to do it, do you?"

"It's not that," Joseph said. "I was just thinking. Remember the time we slept out in a tent in your front yard? Remember how scary it was?"

Owen remembered. He and Joseph had filled the tent with everything they needed to get through the night: pillows, books, popcorn, stuffed animals.

His parents had left the front-porch lights on. The garage light too. It was so bright, it looked like daytime.

It didn't help.

Every little noise sounded like a monster. When Owen's dog, Major, came running around from the back yard, they were sure it was a bear.

They were back in the house by eight-thirty.

"We were in the first grade," Owen said. "Everyone's afraid of the dark in first grade." He hitched his pack higher up on his shoulder. "If you don't want to come, I'll do it by myself."

"I'll come," Joseph said. "I was just remembering."

Owen started walking again. "It'll be so cool. My mom said she has to check with my dad first, but I know he'll say yes. Maybe we can sleep out this weekend, even. Maybe—"

Owen stopped. He put out his hand to stop Joseph. "What's that?"

"What?"

"Shhh." Owen held up a hand for Joseph to listen.

It was voices. They were coming from the direction of the fort.

"There's never anybody else in these woods," Owen said in a low voice.

"Maybe it's Anthony," Joseph whispered. Anthony Petrocelli was in their class. Sometimes he played with them in the fort.

"He went to Florida for spring vacation, remember? Come on. Walk like an Indian."

Owen put down his heel, then the rest of his foot. In a rolling motion. It was the way Indians had walked back in Daniel Boone's time. They could walk miles through the forest without making a single sound.

They may have been quiet, Owen thought, but it must have taken them a long time to get anywhere. No matter how hard he practiced, he could never take more than about two steps before a twig cracked.

Joseph was so close on his heels that he stepped on the back of Owen's sneaker. He was crashing around like a bear. Owen put his finger up to his lips.

As soon as he saw the fort, he stopped. Joseph clutched his arm.

There was no doubt about it.

Someone was in the fort.

Owen heard scuffling noises. Someone laughed. Then there was a shout as a boy's head crashed up through the roof. "Look, Jake, a skylight!"

Someone inside the fort laughed. Then another face appeared in the window.

"Hey!" Owen ran out from behind the trees. "Don't do that! You'll ruin the roof."

The boy looked down at him. He had dark brown hair that fell into his eyes. His head stuck up above the pine branches. So did his shoulders.

He stared at Owen for a split second. Then he disappeared. Owen heard whispering. Then two faces appeared in the window. The boy he had called Jake looked younger. But he had same mean eyes.

They stared down at Owen without saying a word. Then the first boy tossed his head back to get his hair out of his eyes and said, "Oh, yeah? Well, what are you going to do about it?"

"Yeah, little raccoon," Jake said. "What are you going to do about it?" He jabbed the other boy with his elbow. They laughed.

Owen felt his cheeks burning. His heart was pounding in his ears. "That's my fort."

"Did you hear something, Spencer?" said Jake in an innocent voice.

"I don't think so," Spencer said. "Unless that little raccoon down there can talk."

They burst into loud laughs.

Owen felt a tug at his sleeve. "Let's get out of here," Joseph said in a low voice.

Owen yanked his sleeve out of Joseph's grasp.

"That's my fort," he said, louder this time. "Leave it alone."

"*Your* fort?" Spencer held up a pine branch and looked at it. "I don't think so, little raccoon. How could *your* fort be on *our* grandmother's property?"

He tossed the branch out the window. It landed near Owen's feet.

Owen looked down at it.

Their grandmother's property.

He felt a thud in his stomach as if someone had kicked him.

Jake and Spencer were Mrs. Gold's grandsons.

Owen looked back up at them. It was his fort. But it was on their property. And something in their faces told him they didn't want to share.

He didn't know what to do.

"I don't think Grandma would like having someone build a fort on her property. Do you, Jake?" Spencer said.

"I don't think so," Jake said in the same mocking voice. "I think she'd say they were *trespassing*."

Joseph pulled at Owen's sleeve again. "Owen, come on."

Owen glared at them fiercely. "Mrs. Gold said I could use the woods anytime I wanted."

"I think we'd better take this crummy old fort down, don't you?" said Spencer, as if Owen hadn't spoken.

He threw down another pine branch.

This one came so close, Owen had to jump back. His stomach was clenched as tight as his fists.

"Good idea," Jake said.

"But maybe not right away," said Spencer. "Maybe we'll use it for a few days. *Then* we'll wreck it."

"You jerks," Owen said.

"Uh-oh, little raccoon's getting angry," said Spencer. "I hope he doesn't bite."

Jake laughed again.

Owen could feel pressure building up inside him like steam in a volcano. They were in his fort. They were going to wreck it. And there was nothing he could do about it.

He needed to get away. He needed to think.

He spun around. "Come on, Joseph."

"Leaving already?" Jake said.

"Don't worry. I'll be back." Owen didn't turn around. He kept walking. Joseph was right behind him.

"Oh, now I'm *really* scared!" yelled Spencer.

Owen made himself walk slowly. He didn't want to trip. He didn't want them to think he was running away.

He pushed back through the brambles and felt them tear at his jeans. He kept walking.

Joseph caught up to him. "It's okay, Owen, really." He had to jog to keep up. He looked at Owen's face with anxious eyes. "I'll help you. We'll build another one."

Owen stopped so fast, Joseph bumped into him.

"What do you mean, another one?"

When he saw the expression on Owen's face, Joseph took a step back. "If they wreck that one," he said. "I'll help you."

"I don't want another one. I want *this* one." Owen could hardly get the words out. His mouth felt like cement that was hardening. "It's mine."

"I know it is," said Joseph, "but it's on Mrs. Gold's property."

"So?" said Owen. "That doesn't give them the right to destroy it."

"I know." Joseph rubbed his hands together nervously. "Maybe we should tell your mom. She can call Mrs. Gold."

"No!" The word came out like a bullet. "I don't need my mom to solve this. Do you think Daniel Boone asked his mom to solve his problems?"

Joseph didn't say anything.

"I know my mom," Owen said. "She'll say we should talk about it. She thinks talking solves everything. And you saw those guys, Joseph. They don't want to talk. They're jerks. Why should Mrs. Gold do anything? They're her grandsons. Who's going to side against her own grandsons?"

Joseph pulled up his shoulders like a turtle trying to hide its head. "What can we do?"

Owen didn't have a clue.

"I'll think of something," he said.

"Maybe they won't do anything, Owen," Joseph said hopefully. "Maybe they were joking."

"You saw them, Joseph. Kids like that try to ruin things for other kids just to prove how cool they are." Owen started walking. "They'll do something unless we stop them."

"That older kid looked kind of big," Joseph said. He followed Owen around to the front of the house. "Maybe we should wait till they go home. Maybe they won't be here for very long."

Owen sat down on the front steps and put his chin on his hands. He stared straight ahead.

"Hey! Maybe they'll think we went to call the police," Joseph said. His face lit up at the thought. "I bet they're already gone."

"Yeah, right," said Owen.

"They might be, Owen. You don't know."

"I don't?" Owen looked straight into Joseph's eyes. "Okay. Then let's go check." He stood up.

"Check?" The color drained from Joseph's face. "You mean, go back there? You're kidding."

"We have to, Joseph. We can't sit around waiting for them to do whatever they want." Owen tried to block out the picture running in his head: Spencer and Jake in his fort. Tearing down the roof. Knocking down the walls.

Destroying everything.

But he couldn't get it to stop.

"We can't go back right now," Joseph said. He sounded panicky. "We have to think first."

"Okay." Owen looked at his watch. "We'll wait for one hour." He pressed the stopwatch button. The seconds started ticking furiously away. "But then we go back. Okay?"

Joseph still looked pale. But all he said was "Okay."

He didn't say, "What if they're still there?" which was what Owen knew he was thinking. Owen was thinking it too. And he didn't know the answer.

He only knew that they had run away once.

They couldn't run away again.

3

Act Brave and You Are Brave

"Act brave and you are brave." That was another thing Daniel Boone had said. Now Owen knew exactly what it meant.

He kept his eyes on the woods in front of him and walked as purposefully as he could, leading Joseph back across the yard an hour later.

He didn't have to see Joseph's face to know how unhappy he looked. He could feel Joseph behind him, pulling him back. The fort was ahead, pulling him forward.

Every step he took was harder than the one before.

They got to the path. Owen stopped and held

up a hand. He listened as hard as he could. He heard the tops of the pine trees brushing against one another. And crows squawking back and forth.

Nothing else.

He motioned for them to continue. They walked quietly until they saw the fort. The two pine branches were still lying on the ground. Everything else looked the same.

There was no laughter, nothing.

The boys were gone.

Owen felt the air seep out of him. He didn't know he'd been holding his breath.

"See? I told you," Joseph said.

Owen walked toward the fort. The window was still there. The walls were still standing. He broke into a run and was halfway up the ladder before Joseph knew what was happening.

"Hey, wait for me," Joseph yelled.

Owen disappeared inside the fort.

Joseph grabbed the ladder. "Is everything okay?" He started to climb. "I knew they'd get bored. I knew they wouldn't do anything."

Owen could hear the relief in Joseph's voice

as he climbed. He watched as Joseph's red face appeared in the door. He saw Joseph's eyes bug out.

"Wow" was all Joseph said.

The wooden supply box was upside down with the lid torn off. Comic books with ripped covers were scattered all over the floor. Pieces of torn playing cards covered everything like confetti.

There was a huge hole in the roof, and pine needles were everywhere.

The Weapons Wall was empty.

"They crumpled your poem, but at least they didn't tear it." Owen leaned back against the wall and smoothed a piece of paper on his knee. He handed it to Joseph. "It was supposed to be a surprise."

Joseph looked down at the paper and frowned. His dark eyebrows formed a straight line across his forehead. Owen got onto his hands and knees and started putting the comic books into a pile.

Joseph looked up from his poem and watched. Then he crawled over and turned the

supply box right side up. He started to sweep up the pine needles with his hands.

For a few minutes neither one said a word. Then Joseph said, "Do you think they'll come back?"

"You heard them," said Owen. "They said they were going to wreck it, and they will."

Joseph didn't try to argue. "What are we going to do?"

"Make a plan." Owen stopped and looked at Joseph for the first time. Now that the thing he had been so afraid of had actually happened, Owen wasn't afraid anymore. He wasn't even mad. He was calm. Owen couldn't believe how calm he felt.

"A diabolical plan that will teach those guys a lesson," he said.

"What kind of lesson?"

"That you can't come into someone else's environment and wreck it," said Owen. "That you don't have the right to ruin something that someone else worked hard on.

"And if you do," he continued, "you're going to pay for it."

"You're making me nervous, Owen," said Joseph. "What do you mean?"

Owen shrugged, as if what he meant was the most logical thing in the world.

"I mean *war*."

~~~~~~~~~

"I'll be Wolverine and you'll be Badger."

"I will?" Joseph said.

They were in Owen's room. Owen had called Joseph at seven o'clock in the morning and told him to come over right away. He said he had a battle strategy all worked out.

Joseph was sitting on the edge of Owen's bed. Owen was still in his pajamas. His coonskin cap was pulled low on his forehead. The flashlight he had used to read under the covers last night was next to him.

"Those are our secret code names," Owen explained. "We'll use them whenever we want to talk strategy. If I call you up and say, 'Badger? It's Wolverine,' that means you have to get over here right away."

"Okay." Joseph kept his hands on the edge of the bed. He looked as if he were prepared to jump up and run out the door if things got crazy.

Owen held up an orange animal guidebook. "It's perfect, Joseph. Wolverines are small, but they're ferocious. Listen to this."

He flipped through some pages and stopped. "'The ferocious wolverine is perhaps the most powerful mammal for its size. It is capable of driving even a bear or cougar from its kill,'" he read. "'Wolverines prefer carrion but eat anything they can find. They will often hide in a tree and pounce on moose or elk slowed down in heavy snow.'"

He looked up. "Carrion is dead animals. If a wolverine can't find dead ones, it attacks huge live ones. And it's only three feet long." His eyes were shining. "That would be like me attacking a moose. Can you imagine?"

Joseph blinked. "No."

"It says they even raid cabins," Owen said in an awed voice. "One time a wolverine crashed into a hunter's cabin and dragged him outside.

Then it went back in and ate the hunter's food."

He narrowed his eyes. "A wolverine doesn't let *anything* stop it."

"You're a person, Owen, not a wild animal," Joseph said. "That book's talking about animals."

"It's all the same in the wilderness," Owen said in a heavy voice. "Survival of the fittest."

He looked down at his book and started flipping through the pages again. "Wait till you hear about badgers, Joseph. They're perfect for you."

"Owen, I don't think— "

"Here it is." Owen skimmed his finger along a page. "'Fattish body with short legs . . . billows of fat.'"

"Billows?"

"Not that part." Owen ran his finger under the words. "'Badgers move at a clumsy trot and clean themselves frequently. They seldom pick fights, preferring to retreat, if necessary.'"

"I don't retreat. I just don't like to fight, that's all," Joseph said in an injured tone.

"You'll love this part." Owen raised his voice. "'Not many animals are foolish enough to

attack the badger, because it is a formidable adversary, with thick fur, tough hide, and heavy neck muscles.'"

Joseph put his hand up to his neck.

"Isn't that cool? Formidable adversary." Owen snapped the book shut. "We're a perfect combination, Joseph. You barge in and I'll drag them out by their ankles."

He jumped off his bed and grabbed his vest with the fringe on it. "We're ready, Badger."

"I don't feel ready," said Joseph. "That bigger guy looked a lot older than us. Besides, you're small and I'm weak."

"Yeah, but we're smart," Owen said. "That's

the whole idea. You think I'm talking about hand-to-hand combat? No way."

He started looking through a pile of papers on his desk.

"We're going to teach them a lesson, that's all. Kids like that are all over the place. They think they can do whatever they want. But they can't. Not if we use our brains.

"Listen to this." He grabbed a piece of paper and jumped back onto the bed. "We'll start with pine pitch. We can spread it all over the rungs of the ladder."

"Pine pitch is hard to get off," said Joseph. "Mrs. Gold will be mad if they get it all over their clothes."

Owen looked at him. "Joseph. That's the point."

"Oh. Right." Joseph looked embarrassed. "What else?"

"This one's great." Owen tapped his list. "Scat. We'll put it all over the place."

"Gross." Joseph made a face. "That stuff's got germs."

"We don't have to touch it. We'll use

Major's pooper-scooper," Owen said. "We'll get the dry, stale stuff. Those wimps will get one look at it and run. Who wants to hang around when your hands are sticky and there's poop everywhere?"

"I guess," Joseph said. He didn't sound convinced.

"Here's another one. We'll cut through some of the rungs on the ladder," Owen said. "When they try to climb, the rungs'll break."

"I don't think that's a good idea," Joseph said. "If they get hurt, we'll get in trouble."

Owen thought for a minute. "Yeah, you're right." He scribbled something on his list. "If they tell anyone, we have to look like innocent defenders. We'll just cut one near the bottom to annoy them."

"We'd better not make them too mad, Owen," Joseph said. "They'll wreck the fort even more."

"I already know that," said Owen. "That's why we have to have one *really good* thing. Something to scare them away once and for all."

"Like what?"

"A snake. Maybe a poisonous one."

"No way!" Joseph jumped to his feet. "I hate snakes—you know that. I don't even like pictures of them. This is where I draw the line, Owen. You're going too far."

"Okay, okay, calm down," Owen said. "Not a poisonous one. Those guys won't know the difference, anyway. Actually, I was thinking more of a garter snake. They're harmless."

There were small beads of sweat on Joseph's forehead. "What are you going to do with it?"

"I was thinking we could put it in a bag and leave it in the fort. If they start to wreck things, they'll tear it open, see the snake, and freak out."

"We?" said Joseph.

"I'll take care of the snake—don't worry."

"When are we going to do all this?" Joseph said in a faint voice.

"We'd better start right away," Owen said. "Get out there early, before they do."

"I have to go home first," said Joseph. "I didn't

eat breakfast. My mother said I had to by home by eight o'clock, or else."

Owen didn't know how Joseph could even think about food at a time like this. But eating made Joseph happy. Maybe it would calm him down.

"Okay, but hurry up. I'll start looking for scat on my way to the fort." Owen began putting on his sneakers. "Meet me out there as soon as you can."

"You're going to the fort? By yourself?"

From the sound of Joseph's voice, Owen knew it wouldn't take much to make Joseph jump ship. He stood up and put his hand on Joseph's shoulder.

"Joseph. It's going to be fine. This plan is great. It can't fail."

"Are you sure?"

"Sure I'm sure." Owen gave Joseph's shoulder a little shake. "Act brave and you are brave, remember?"

"How do we know it works?" said Joseph.

"Because Daniel Boone said so, okay?"

"Okay," Joseph said reluctantly.

Owen bent back down to tie his shoe. "Anyway, those guys aren't even awake yet. Kids like that get up at ten o'clock."

"Yeah. I guess." Joseph opened the door. "I'll be back as soon as I can."

"Over and out, Badger," said Owen.

"Over and out, Wolverine," Joseph said. "Bye."

4

Nope, Can't Be Here

"You two were awfully busy up there," said Mrs. Foote. Owen's mom looked up from her desk and smiled.

He kept walking toward the kitchen.

"Owen?"

He turned around and walked back to the door of the study. "What?"

His mom gave him a puzzled frown. "That was kind of rude."

"I'm going to my fort," Owen said. If he was going to go, he had to go now. He couldn't stop, or he might never go.

"Like that?" said his mom.

Owen looked down. He felt a flush of anger spread over his face. "What do you want, Mom? I'm busy."

Mrs. Foote's eyes were searching his face as if she thought she'd find words written on his forehead.

Owen gave a huge sigh so she would know how impatient she was making him.

"I wanted to tell you that Mrs. Gold called," his mom said slowly. "She's going to stop by this afternoon with her two grandsons so you can meet them. They're visiting from New York City for their spring vacation."

"This afternoon?" Owen slammed his palm against the door. "No way. I don't want to meet her stupid grandsons."

His mom sat back as if he'd slammed his hand right in front of her face. She looked shocked. "You don't even know them, Owen."

"You always do this to me, Mom." Owen could feel his eyes stinging. "You always accept invitations for me to play with dumb kids I don't even know. Then you talk to the mother and I have to play with the dumb kids."

He was pacing back and forth between the door and the couch. He felt trapped, like an animal in the zoo. "No way. I'm busy. Nope, can't be here. Sorry."

He kept hitting the back of the couch with his hand.

"Owen, what is *wrong* with you?" His mom's voice sounded half mad and half worried. "All they're going to do is stop by and say hello."

Owen knew he couldn't look at her face or he might tell her everything. "I'm not going to do it, Mom. Joseph and I have plans. Call Mrs. Gold and tell her not to come."

"I can't. They were going to Candlewood Lake to swim and have a picnic. They're going to stop by here on their way home."

There was a small silence. Then: "I don't know why you're so upset," she said in a gentle voice.

"You don't know anything, Mom, that's the problem."

Owen felt his eyes start to water. "You think

just because I'm a kid, I should like every other kid. You think that if the mother's nice, then the kid will be nice. You think you can tell me what to do all the time. Everyone thinks they can boss me around like I'm a baby. But I'm not."

"Who's everyone, Owen?" his mom asked quietly. "I only—"

Owen turned and walked stiffly out of the room.

"Owen, come back here."

Owen didn't stop. He walked up the stairs and closed his door. He went over to his dresser and took out a pair of jeans and a T-shirt. He took off his pajama top and started to pull the shirt over his head.

He moved carefully so he wouldn't make any mistakes. He was mad about so many things, he didn't know which way to turn.

He was mad at his mom.

He was mad at Mrs. Gold's grandsons.

He was mad at himself for almost crying, down there in the study.

And suddenly he was absolutely furious at his shirt.

He had pulled out the one with the neck that was too small. The one that got stuck halfway over his head. The way it was now.

The harder he pulled, the more it felt like a tourniquet around his skull.

He wanted to rip it off and tear it into a million pieces.

"Stupid shirt!" he shouted.

He stumbled blindly around his room, trying to pull it off. He crashed into his bed and fell onto the floor.

With one final yank the T-shirt came off. Owen lay on the floor, panting.

"When you find yourself yelling at a shirt, maybe it's time to reexamine your whole life, Owen."

His sister, Lydia, was standing in the doorway. She had her sixth-grade know-it-all face on. The one that meant she knew everything and Owen knew nothing.

"Get out of here!" He hurled the shirt at her head.

Lydia caught it with one hand and raised her right eyebrow. "Maybe you should get help."

Owen lunged toward the door to slam it. "Go away!"

He yanked open his drawer, took out another shirt, and pulled it over his head. Then he put on his coonskin cap and slung his pack over his shoulder.

He opened his door a crack. The hall was empty.

Owen crept down the hall to his parents' bedroom and picked up the phone.

"Trent residence. Joseph speaking."

"It's Wolverine."

"Hi, O—" Joseph caught himself just in time. "Badger speaking," he said in a tense whisper.

"Meet me at the fort. Now."

"Why? What happened?"

But Owen had already hung up. He tiptoed down the stairs and past the study. The door was closed. He could hear his mom and Lydia talking inside.

Owen ran out to the garage and grabbed Major's pooper-scooper and a bucket. Then he headed out for the woods.

He would worry about his mom later.

The enemy was at Candlewood Lake.

There wasn't a minute to lose.

~~~~~~~~~~

"Owen, are you up there?"

Joseph's tense voice came from the bottom of the ladder.

Owen dumped the last of the scat on the floor of the fort and crawled to the doorway. "I'm coming down."

He threw the pooper-scooper and the bucket to the ground and started down the ladder. "I found a lot of scat. It must have been a raccoon's. It had a lot of raspberry seeds in it."

Joseph looked nervous, but he was wearing his raccoon cap. He raised the shovel he was holding.

"Remember that hole you dug last year to trap a rabbit?" he said to Owen. "The one you put carrots in and covered over with sticks?"

"Yeah." Owen jumped and landed on the ground next to him.

"Well, I was thinking," Joseph said. "I could

dig a real big hole on the path they come down and cover it over. I looked up badgers in a book. They're powerful burrowers, you know. They can outpace a man with a shovel."

"Cool."

"You know how you can tell a badger's burrow from other animals'?"

"How?"

"A badger's burrow will probably have rattlesnake rattles around it," said Joseph. "Can you believe it? Badgers eat rattlesnakes. They're actually fond of them, my book said."

"Really? Does that mean you want to be the one who gets the snake?"

Joseph shrugged. "Only if it's a rattler."

When Owen laughed, so did Joseph. Then Joseph's face got serious again. "What if they come back while we're here?"

"They won't." Owen started looking around for a stick to scrape the pitch with. "They're swimming at Candlewood Lake."

"How do you know?"

"My mom talked to Mrs. Gold. She's bringing

them to our house this afternoon to meet me."

"You're kidding." Joseph's mouth fell open. "To your house? Today? What did you say? Did you tell your mom?"

"Nope. I told her she could have them over, but I wouldn't be there."

"What did she say?"

"I don't know." Owen bent over to pick up a stick. "I didn't wait around. I went up to my room."

"Wow." Joseph stared at Owen's back. He knew how strict Owen's mom was. If Owen walked out on her in the middle of a conversation, he was in trouble.

Joseph knew it would take something very important to make Owen leave while his mom was talking to him.

"I had to," said Owen, as if he had read Joseph's mind. "Sometimes there are things you have to do. My dad says it's okay to do what you have to, as long as you're willing to accept the consequences."

"What do you think the consequences will be?"

"I'm not sure, but at least the fort will be safe."

"Yeah, and if those guys get mad and come looking for you, you'll be safe," said Joseph. "You'll be in your room for the rest of the vacation."

"Maybe," Owen said. "But it'll be worth it."

"Yeah." Joseph started down the path with his shovel. "Boy, those guys are sure going to be sorry they messed around with a wolverine and a badger."

"You can say that again," said the wolverine.

5

The Most Important Thing
in the World

"Where were you? It's almost dinner time."

"My fort."

Owen was standing inside the kitchen door. His mom was stirring something in a pot on the stove. Owen could tell she had been waiting for him.

"You put me in a very embarrassing position this afternoon, Owen."

Owen didn't say anything.

"Something's going on here, and I don't know what it is." His mom stopped stirring and looked at him. "The way you flew off the handle this morning was uncalled for."

"I didn't want to meet them," said Owen.

"But why?" Mrs. Foote's voice rose. "What's the big deal about saying hello to two boys you don't know? I had to stand in our driveway and say that you hadn't gotten back from Joseph's yet. In other words, lie, Owen. Maybe it was only a white lie, but it was still a lie."

"Mom . . ."

"I thought we had a better relationship than that. I thought we talked about things."

Owen shifted his weight from one foot to the other. He had expected his mom to be mad. But she didn't sound mad. She sounded hurt.

"Hi." Mr. Foote opened the door from the garage. He looked at his wife's face. Then at Owen. "Did I interrupt something?"

"I don't want to talk about it," Mrs. Foote said.

Mr. Foote raised his eyebrows and looked at Owen. "Owen?"

"Me neither."

Mr. Foote put his briefcase down on the counter. "Well, this is a fine how-do-you-do. I come home from a hard day at work to find a dark cloud hanging over my house, and no one wants to talk about it."

Lydia walked in and sat down at the table. "Owen walked out when Mom was talking to him and she had to lie to Mrs. Gold and he's doing something sneaky, but he won't tell what."

"Be quiet," Owen said through clenched teeth.

"Lydia, please set the table," their mom said.

Lydia made a face, but she got up and started taking forks and knives out of the drawer. Mr. Foote went over and kissed his wife on the cheek. "Why don't we all sit down and eat, and maybe Owen will tell us what's going on. Okay, Owen?"

After Mrs. Foote served the food, they all sat down and started to eat. Except Owen. He was too busy thinking about the best way to tell the story.

He wanted to tell it so his dad would side with him, not with his mom. And so his mom would see that *she* was the one who had put *him* in an awkward spot. And so they would all see that he really *had* to booby-trap the fort, even if it meant touching poop, which he knew would give his mom a fit.

But there was no time to think. They were all chewing and watching and waiting for him to say something. So Owen told it the way it had happened, from the beginning.

And the way he told it, the story did all the things he wanted.

No one interrupted. Every once in a while his dad gave a short laugh. Or his mom drew in a sharp breath. But when she asked, "Oh, Owen, did you wash your hands?" Mr. Foote put his hand on her arm and said, "Let him finish."

Even Lydia didn't barge in. She just kept saying things like "Those jerks" and "I'd kill them" in a low voice.

He couldn't believe how good it felt to tell the whole story. When Lydia said, "You're crazy, you know that?" he felt even better.

He could tell she was impressed.

All his dad said was "I don't think you gave your mother enough credit, Owen. I think that if you'd told her about the boys in the first place, all this could have been avoided."

"I couldn't, Dad." Owen turned to his mom. "You're an OPM, Mom, you know you are. You would have wanted to call Mrs. Gold so we could talk about it."

"OPM?" said Mr. Foote.

"Over-Protective Mother," Lydia said.

"Yeah, Mom's a VOPM," said Owen.

"That's because she loves you," his dad said.

"Yeah, but sometimes she loves me too much," Owen said in a glum voice.

"I think there are worse things than having a mother who worries about you, Owen," said Mr. Foote.

Mrs. Foote finally spoke up. "What's *wrong* with calling Mrs. Gold? I think if we got everyone together to talk about this, we could straighten the whole thing out."

"These aren't the kind of kids who want to talk things out, Mom," Owen said. "If they were, they wouldn't be doing something mean in the first place."

"Owen's right," said Lydia. "Remember Judy Benedict? That girl who kept bothering me in fifth grade? One day she poured her milk all over my lunch tray. You called her mother to talk about it. The next day she poured her milk in my lap."

Owen couldn't believe it. Lydia had said he was right. She was actually standing up for him.

"Anyway, it's my problem," Owen said. "I want to solve it my own way."

"Let him do it, Mom," Lydia said. "His way might work."

Mr. Foote stood up. "Honey, I think that if we're lucky enough to get a consensus from these two, we had better consider it very seriously."

He pulled out Mrs. Foote's chair. "As long as you two are getting along so well, your mother and I are going to watch the news while you clean up."

Lydia didn't even object. She made Owen tell

her his plan again while she washed the pots and he loaded the dishwasher. "What do you think they'll do?" she said. She put the last pot in the drying rack.

"I'm not sure," said Owen. "That's why I have to watch. If they go nuts, I'll have to do something."

"Watch? *You're* nuts, Owen. What if they see you?"

"They won't. Joseph and I built a duck blind. Like hunters use. They won't be able to see anything."

"Mom will never let you," Lydia said.

"I'm not going to tell her, and you can't, either. You have to promise."

They looked at each other. The top of Owen's head barely came up to Lydia's shoulder. His sharp collarbones stuck out under his T-shirt. His arms looked as if they would snap as easily as twigs.

But something in his face made it look strong.

"Okay, I promise," Lydia said, "but I hope you know what you're doing."

Owen gave a sheepish grin. "Me too."

~~~~~~~~

By the time his mom came upstairs, he was lying on his back under the covers with his arms behind his head.

"You're in bed early." She came over and sat down on his bed. "I'm sorry the boys hurt your fort, Owen."

"Don't worry. I'll get back at them."

His mom opened her mouth to say something more.

Owen sat up. "You don't understand, Mom. That fort's the most important thing in the world to me. It's mine. I built it. I like it better than this house, even. When I get out of college, I'll probably live in it for a few years."

His mom laughed.

"I'm not joking."

"I know you're not, Owen." She looked as if she were trying to put her thoughts into words Owen would listen to. And understand.

"Don't worry." Owen lay back down. "I'm

not going to mess around with those guys. You should see them. One of them looks about fifteen. I bet they both have their black belts in karate too. They have to, living in New York City. There are a lot of muggers in New York, you know."

His mom laughed again. "You think of everything, don't you?" She rubbed his cheek with the back of her hand. "Maybe you're right. Maybe I don't have to worry about you so much anymore."

"You will anyway, Mom, but you're getting better."

His mom kissed him. "I do have to say one thing, Owen. Do you see how complicated and murky things get when you don't tell the truth?"

"Yeah."

"Life is complicated enough as it is," his mom said. "We have to be able to trust one another."

"Okay."

Mrs. Foote turned off the light and went to the door.

"Did you know wolverines are the most

powerful mammals for their size?" Owen said suddenly.

"No." His mom stopped. "Why?"

"I was just thinking." Owen rolled over onto his side and closed his eyes. "I love you, Mom."

"I love you too, Owen."

She waited for a moment. But Owen didn't say anything more.

So she left, shutting the door behind her.

6

This Is Still My Kingdom!

"I don't feel so good."

"It's about time you got here." Owen jumped off the front steps and picked up the paper bag at his side. "Come on."

He didn't look at Joseph's worried face. Or at Joseph's hand on his stomach.

Joseph followed him around the corner of the house.

"My mother almost didn't let me come," he said to Owen's back. "When I couldn't eat my breakfast, she put her hand on my forehead. She wanted to get the thermometer."

Owen kept walking toward the woods.

"What's in the bag?" Joseph said.

"The snake."

"What kind is it?"

"Garter." Owen looked back over his shoulder. "You know the one who lives under our back porch? The one I kept in my aquarium last summer? I went out this morning and caught him again. I think he recognized me."

"How could you tell?"

"When I looked him in the eyes and told him about the plan, he looked back like he knew me."

Owen stopped in front of a huge pile of branches. "You get in," he told Joseph. "I have to put this in the fort."

"Don't leave me," Joseph said in a panicky voice. "What if they come? What if they see me?"

"They won't," Owen said. "Why do you think we made the duck blind? Just stay on your stomach and you'll be safe. I'll be right back."

"Hurry." Joseph crawled into the blind. "Can you see me?"

Owen walked to the bottom of the ladder and

looked back. "Nope." He looked up at his fort. It looked far away. He took a deep breath and started to climb. He was careful not to touch the pine pitch. Or step on the broken rung.

When he got inside, he crawled over to the corner, avoiding the scat, and put the bag down. Then he started back toward the door.

That's when he heard voices.

Owen froze. His eyes darted back and forth between the window and the door.

There was no doubt about it.

They were coming.

Owen could hear their footsteps on the path. He heard them laughing.

He thought about Joseph, alone in the duck blind. He wondered who was more scared.

Joseph or him.

One of the boys said something that made the other one laugh. Owen looked around the fort. It was too late to escape, and there was nowhere to hide.

For the first time, being in his fort didn't make him feel safe.

It made him feel cornered.

A loud crash made him almost jump through the roof.

"Whoa!" a voice shouted.

Then there was another crash and the sound of something thrashing around. It sounded as if a large animal had fallen into a trap.

Joseph's hole! Owen leaned back against the wall of the fort and closed his eyes.

"Hey, get off me!" he heard Spencer yell in an angry voice.

"I can't help it." Jake sounded mad too.

There was more thrashing. And a bit of grunting.

"What *is* this thing?" Owen could hear sticks being thrown around.

Then, "Someone dug a hole." It was Jake's voice. "Probably that raccoon boy and his friend."

"Yeah, well, they'll be sorry," Spencer said. "Wait till they see what we do to their precious fort."

Their footsteps came closer.

Owen bit his lip and thought about the other booby traps he and Joseph had set. His heart sank.

They weren't diabolical. They were stupid.

Stupid, baby traps.

They wouldn't scare kids like Spencer and Jake. They would only make them mad. Those kids would get all the way up to the fort, all right.

And when they got there, they'd see him, Owen. Alone.

Owen swallowed. His mouth was full of water, the way it got when he was about to throw up.

The footsteps stopped under the fort.

"Maybe we'd better not," Jake said. "That kid says he knows Grandma. What if he tells her?"

"So? We'll be back in New York."

"Come on, Spencer, let's get out of here. Who cares about a dumb old fort, anyway? I don't want to spend my last day doing this. Let's go swimming."

"You're just chicken." The fort shook as

Spencer grabbed the ladder. Owen pressed his back against the wall.

"I'm not letting those punks get away with this," Spencer went on. "I'll go up myself."

The fort shook again.

"What the—?" Spencer said. "There's sticky stuff all over this thing."

Owen heard a swear word.

"It doesn't come off, either."

"Come on, Spencer, let's go."

Owen's eyes were glued to the open doorway.

The fort shook again. Harder this time.

There was another swear word.

"You broke it, Spencer."

"I didn't break it. Someone cut through it."

"I told you those kids were weird," Jake said. "The whole fort's probably rigged. I'm leaving— I mean it."

"Not me."

Owen didn't like the sound of Spencer's voice. His eyes frantically searched the fort for something. Anything.

The bag.

Owen opened the bag as carefully as he could so it wouldn't make a sound. He got up on his knees.

"See you later, Spencer," Jake shouted from a distance.

"Go ahead, chicken!" Spencer yelled.

Spencer started to climb again. Owen could hear him getting higher and higher. In another second he'd be at the top.

Owen held up the snake and looked him straight in the eye.

"Sorry about this," he mouthed.

He put the snake on the floor near the door and gave him a gentle nudge. The snake slithered forward and disappeared over the edge.

"What the—? Hey! Get off me!"

There was a high-pitched scream and the sound of a body hitting the ground.

"Spencer!" Owen heard the fear in Jake's voice. He heard Jake running, then his worried voice under the fort.

"What happened? What is it?"

"A stupid snake." Spencer's voice was shaking.

"Did it bite you?"

"No."

"Where did it go?"

"Into those bushes over there."

"What if it was poisonous?" Jake's voice rose higher. "What if there are more up there?"

"There aren't any poisonous snakes around here."

"Oh, yeah? What about what Grandma said? She said to watch out for copperheads, remember? I'm leaving. I'm not kidding anymore."

Owen heard him walking away.

"Okay, wait up, Jake," Spencer called. "I'm bored with this dumb fort. Wait up!"

The sound of their footsteps got fainter and fainter. Then Owen couldn't hear them at all.

He sagged back against the wall of the fort and closed his eyes. He stayed that way for a long time, listening to the silence. The warm smell of pine was all around him.

A crow cawed in the distance. A second crow answered back.

Owen heard a tense whisper. "Owen!"

He crawled to the door and leaned out. "What?"

There was a rustling noise. Joseph's head popped up from behind the blind. The boys stared at each other.

Seeing how scared Joseph looked made Owen realize how scared he, Owen, had been.

But not anymore.

He stood up on the front porch. "Could you see what happened when the snake hit him?" he asked in a loud voice.

"Yeah." Joseph ran over and stood looking up at him.

"What was it like?"

Joseph's face broke into a huge smile. "Awesome."

"*Ya-hoo!*" Owen shouted. He jumped off the porch and landed on the ground in a crouch. Then he sprang to his feet and grabbed Joseph around the shoulders.

The two of them jumped up and down and around and around in circles.

When they were exhausted, they fell in a heap

on the ground. "I was never so scared in my entire life," Joseph panted.

"Me neither."

"Do you think they'll come back?"

"No way."

"Spencer was at the top."

"I know."

"You should have seen his face."

"Was it great?"

Joseph nodded. "Yeah."

Owen grinned. Then grabbed his hat by its tail and tossed it as high as he could into the air.

"This is still my kingdom!" he shouted.

"Mine too!" shouted Joseph. He tossed his hat. "Mine too!"

7

Spencer and Jake Gold, This Is Owen Foote

Owen's mom said they could spend the night in the fort. She even told Owen she'd take him to the store to buy some junk food.

They were halfway down the snack aisle when she stopped.

"Oh, no," she said.

"A deal's a deal, Mom." Owen tossed a bag of potato chips into the cart. He reached for another one of popcorn. "You said two kinds."

"Owen." Owen's mom moved in front of him, blocking his view. "Mrs. Gold is at the end of the aisle with her grandsons."

Owen's hand froze in midair. "Are you joking?"

His mom shook her head.

Owen peered around her.

"Oh, my gosh." He ducked back behind her again. What if they had told their grandmother everything? What if she was mad at him?

Owen grabbed his mom's sleeve. "What should I do?"

There wasn't time to plan. Mrs. Gold had spotted them and was coming down the aisle toward them.

"Owen," he heard her call.

His mom turned around to face her. "Mary. What a surprise."

Owen stepped out from behind his mom. "Hi, Mrs. Gold."

Spencer and Jake were standing on either side of her. They looked as if they had seen a ghost.

The ghost was him. Owen could see it in their faces. Owen Foote, the kid their grandmother wanted them to meet, was the same kid they'd called "little raccoon."

Except that Owen wasn't a raccoon. He was a wolverine. It was too bad for them that they hadn't known the difference.

Looking at them now, Owen realized they were a lot more nervous than he was. If Mrs. Gold knew what they had done to his fort, she'd be mad, all right.

But not at Owen. At Spencer and Jake. And all three of them knew it.

Owen felt a huge grin spread across his face. "How are you doing, Mrs. Gold?"

"I'm so glad we ran into you, Owen," she said. "I wanted you to meet my grandsons before they left. Spencer and Jake Gold, this is Owen Foote."

Spencer was staring at the floor. Jake looked as if he were trying to grind a hole in the tile with the toe of his sneaker.

Owen stuck out his hand so fast, he nearly jabbed Spencer in the nose. "Hi, Spencer," he said in a hearty voice.

Spencer had to look at him. His eyes were as slitty as a snake's. He put out his hand and pulled it back again the moment it touched Owen's.

But not before Owen could see the dark brown pitch stains all over it.

His grin got wider.

"Hi, Jake," he said in his new, big voice. He knew he sounded like a politician running for office. But he wasn't worried about the outcome.

He knew he had already won.

Jake mumbled something. Mrs. Gold poked him in the middle of his back. "Jake?"

Jake shook Owen's hand. He looked embarrassed.

"We're buying things for the boys' lunch before I take them to the airport," Mrs. Gold said to Mrs. Foote. She looked at Owen. "I'm sorry we missed you yesterday."

"Me too," Owen said. "I was hoping I could show Spencer and Jake my tree fort. I never told you, Mrs. Gold, but I built a tree fort in your woods. I hope you don't mind."

"Mind? I'm delighted," said Mrs. Gold. "Jake

and Spencer's father practically lived in tree forts when he was your age."

"Maybe Jake and Spencer can come and see it sometime," Owen said. "The roof needs some repair work, but it's really great."

"My grandsons live in New York City," said Mrs. Gold. "I think they're probably more comfortable on the subway than in the woods, aren't you, boys?"

The way they were shuffling around, Owen could tell they wished they were underground right now.

"That's okay." Owen gave his hearty laugh. "I'll toughen them up."

Spencer's eyes were boring holes in him like laser beams.

But it didn't hurt; it tickled. Owen felt like laughing.

Mrs. Foote put her hand on Owen's shoulder and gave it a firm squeeze. "I'm afraid Owen and I have to get going, Mary. It was very nice to meet you boys. I hope you have a safe trip home."

"Bye, Jake. Bye, Spencer," Owen said. He turned around and grabbed the cart. His mom kept her hand on his shoulder while she walked beside him.

"That was quite a performance you put on, Owen," she said. "I bet you'd win an Academy Award for that one."

"What do you mean, Mom?" said Owen. "I was being polite."

He shook his head as if he had bad news to tell her. "Mrs. Gold really ought to work on those guys. Their handshakes are like wet rags."

"Sometimes you amaze me," said his mom. "You really do."

"Sometimes you amaze me too," said Owen. He put on a serious face. "We don't really have to get going, do we?"

She looked straight at him. "I couldn't stand to watch you torture those poor boys for one more minute."

"I guess it was only a white lie," Owen said. "A very small one."

His mom narrowed her eyes. "Owen . . ."

Owen put one foot on the back rung of the cart. "That's okay, Mom. I know you did it for humanitarian reasons."

Then, before she could say another word, he pushed off with his other foot and cruised down the aisle.

He didn't have to see his mom's face to know what it looked like.

Imagining it was great enough.

8

It's a Bear

"There's even a chapter that tells you how to make a blowgun," Owen said.

He pulled a book out of his pack and threw it onto his sleeping bag. "Boy, I wish we had had a blowgun. We could have loaded in some peas and *ppffffftt!*" He held his fingers up to his mouth and blew. "Bull's-eye!"

"I think they're illegal," said Joseph, "except in South America." He was on his hands and knees, smoothing out his sleeping bag.

"Not unless you use poison darts," said Owen. He tore open a bag of potato chips. "We could hunt birds with them. That wouldn't be

illegal. There's a chapter on practical taxidermy too. Skinning and stuffing."

"Skinning and stuffing?" Joseph patted his pillow into place. "I don't think I'm ready for that."

"When you live in the wilderness, you have to do a lot of skinning and stuffing," said Owen. "Where do you think this came from?"

He took off his coonskin cap and hung it on a nail in the wall.

"I try not to think about it," said Joseph.

Owen crammed a handful of potato chips into his mouth. "Wouldn't it have been great, living back in the days of Daniel Boone? Sleeping out in a fort, hunting for food, and cooking over a fire?"

"I don't think that's all they did," said Joseph. "I think it was a lot of hard work. You always read about kids having to chop wood and plow the fields and stuff. And lots of times they got kidnapped by Indians."

He looked out at the woods. "Are you sure your mom will remember to leave the garage light on?"

"I'm sure," Owen said. "Knowing her, she'll probably check on us a thousand times, anyway."

Joseph pulled something out of his pack.

"Pajamas?" said Owen.

"My mother made me bring them." Joseph looked at Owen's face. "I wasn't going to wear them."

He stuffed them back into his pack.

Owen crawled into his sleeping bag. "Your mom is even more overprotective than mine."

"I know."

"They could start an OPM club."

"Yeah."

It was almost dark. Owen turned on his flashlight. "Look." He pressed the light into the palm of his hand. Through his pinkish skin they could see his dark veins and pale bones.

"What about this?" Joseph turned on his light and held it up under his chin. It made his face look very spooky.

Owen burrowed farther into his bag. "I'm going to live out here after college, Joseph. You

can too, if you want. We could have a great time."

Joseph got into his sleeping bag. "I don't know. I'm not as crazy about the woods as you are, Owen. They make me kind of nervous sometimes."

"But you love nature and flowers and stuff," said Owen. "I could catch the food and you could grow things. You could write poems too. Lots of people write poems about nature."

"Yeah, I really like poetry," Joseph said. "I think I might be a poet when I grow up. Then I wouldn't have to worry about spelling and punctuation."

"I know what you mean."

They lay on their backs and made zigzag patterns on the roof and walls with their flashlights. They ate all the potato chips and most of the popcorn.

Finally Owen said, "On the count of three, let's turn off our flashlights, okay?"

"Okay."

They held them still.

"One, two, three."

There were two clicks, then darkness.

Very dark darkness.

Owen stared up into the black and blinked. He could feel Joseph beside him. It was so quiet, it was almost loud.

"What was that?" Joseph said suddenly.

"What?"

"That."

Owen listened. "I don't hear anything."

"I do. I think it's a bear." Joseph clicked on his flashlight. He was sitting straight up. Owen sat up beside him.

Joseph was right. Something was coming down the path, headed in their direction.

They heard heavy footsteps.

"Boys?" Mr. Foote's voice came from under the fort.

"Dad!" Owen scrambled for the doorway. Joseph was right behind him. Owen shone his light down on his dad's face.

"Your mother wanted me to bring this out to you," Mr. Foote said. He held something up in the air.

"Actually, first she made me go out and *buy* it, then she made me bring it out," he said. "You know Mom."

A bright light flooded the woods. "It's a battery-powered tent light," said Mr. Foote. "It'll last you all night if you want, but it might make it a little hard to fall asleep."

"That's okay." Owen leaned out over the front porch to grab it. "If it makes Mom feel better, we'll take it."

"You boys all right out here?"

"Yeah, great."

"Have a good time, then. The back door will be unlocked if you need anything."

"Okay. Night, Dad."

"Night, Mr. Foote."

"Good night, boys."

They listened to his footsteps fade away. Then Owen put the light on the floor near his head and got back into his sleeping bag.

The fort was as bright as day.

"I guess we could leave it on for a little bit," Owen said.

"Sure," Joseph said. "Why not?"

"I'll turn it off in a few minutes." Owen gave a huge yawn and closed his eyes.

When he opened them again, seconds later, the light was still shining.

And so was the sun.

It was morning.